# SAMMY SPIDER'S
# FIRST
## DAY OF SCHOOL

Sylvia A. Rouss

Illustrated by
Katherine Janus Kahn

KAR-BEN
PUBLISHING

*To Derek and Hayden, who take delight in all God's creatures —S.A.R.*

*To all the wonderful "Miss Sarahs," especially my cousin Harriet Weintraub, my niece Mandy Voyda, and my friend Jacqueline Jules —K.J.K.*

Text copyright © 2009 by Sylvia A. Rouss
Illustrations copyright © 2009 by Katherine Janus Kahn

KAR-BEN PUBLISHING
A division of Lerner Publishing Group, Inc.
241 First Avenue North
Minneapolis, MN 55401 U.S.A.
1-800-4-Karben

Website address: www.karben.com


Library of Congress Cataloging-in-Publication Data

Rouss, Sylvia A.
    Sammy Spider's first day of school / by Sylvia A. Rouss ;
illustrated by Katherine Janus Kahn.
        p.   cm.
    Summary: Sammy Spider sneaks onto Josh's lunch box and
accompanies him to school, where he learns about the important
Jewish value of being kind to animals.
    ISBN 978–0–8225–8583–1 (lib. bdg. : alk. paper)
    [1. Judaism—Fiction.  2. Schools—Fiction.  3. Spiders—Fiction.]
    I. Kahn, Katherine, ill.  II. Title.
PZ7.R7622Sad  2009
[E]—dc22                                                    2007047769

Manufactured in the United States of America
1 2 3 4 5 6 – PA – 14 13 12 11 10 09

Sammy Spider was dangling from his web on the kitchen ceiling when he heard Mrs. Shapiro calling Josh. "It's time for school!"

"Can I go to school, too?"
Sammy asked his mother.

"Silly little Sammy," she
answered. "Spiders don't go
to school. Spiders spin webs."

Sammy lowered himself on a strand of webbing and perched on the lunchbox near Josh's backpack.

"Don't forget your lunch," Mrs. Shapiro reminded Josh.

He tucked his lunchbox into his backpack. He didn't notice Sammy.

Mrs. Spider sighed. "I guess my little Sammy is going to school after all."

Inside the backpack,
Sammy shuddered
"It's dark in here.
I hope we get
there soon."

"We're here!" announced Mrs. Shapiro, as she pulled into the school parking lot. She helped Josh out of the car and walked him to his classroom.

"*Boker Tov!*
Good morning!"
Miss Sarah
welcomed Josh.

"You're just in time for opening circle." Josh took his lunch box out of the backpack and put it in his cubby. He joined his classmates on the rug. Sammy climbed down and followed.

The children listened as Miss Sarah read a book about Noah's Ark.

"Noah brought two of every animal onto the ark to save them from the great flood," she said. "How do you think he took care of them?"

"He fed them." Jordan answered. "He made sure they stayed dry."

"Except when he was giving them a bath," Gabby added.

"He touched them gently so they wouldn't get scared," replied Josh.

"I like your answers. You're really thinking," said Miss Sarah. "Do any of you have pets at home?"

"I have a hamster," responded Jordan. "I feed him and help clean his cage."

"My dog likes to play catch with me," said Todd.

"My kitten purrs when I rub the back of her neck," giggled Shannon.

"Why doesn't Josh tell them about me?" Sammy wondered.

"It sounds like you already know something about an important Jewish value — kindness to animals," Miss Sarah told them.

"Josh, would you like to feed the goldfish today?" she asked, handing him a small container of food. "Then you can join your friends."

Sammy watched Josh carefully sprinkle food into the fish bowl. A little bit fell to the floor. He tasted it. "Yuck!" he exclaimed. "I'm glad I'm not a fish."

"It's a good thing children don't have eight legs," Sammy said to himself, dodging their feet as they hurried to the activity centers.

He followed Josh to the easel. Josh put on a smock, picked up a large brush, and began to paint. A few drops splattered onto Sammy's head.

"Josh, come help me," called Shannon, who was making a tall tower of blocks.

"Sure," he answered. "Let's build Noah's ark."

Sammy wiped off the paint and crawled over to watch.

Suddenly, the blocks came tumbling down, and Sammy scurried away just in time. He was glad when Miss Sarah announced clean-up.

At snack time, Miss Sarah gave each child a slice of banana and some animal crackers.

"Wow! It looks like Noah's ark!" exclaimed Sammy, as he watched Josh line up his animals on the banana boat. "Where's my snack?" he wondered, and then he remembered, "Spiders don't eat bananas. Spiders spin webs."

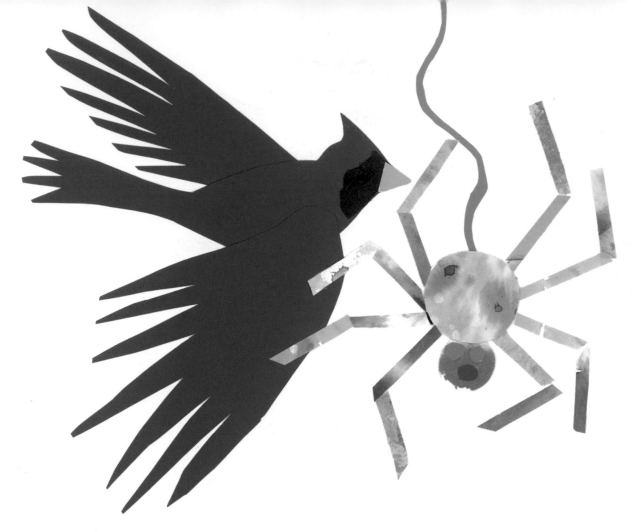

After snack, it was time to go outside. "Who
wants to help put seeds in our bird feeder?"
asked Miss Sarah. Sammy looked out the
window and saw two large birds swoop down
into the play yard. He decided to stay inside.

Sammy watched Josh hang upside down on
the bars. "I can do that too," Sammy thought,
dangling from a silky strand of webbing.

Miss Sarah smiled when Gabby picked up a snail
and brought it to her. Sammy couldn't hear what
Miss Sarah said, but he saw Gabby put the snail
back into the flowerbed.

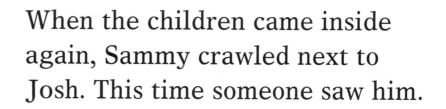

When the children came inside again, Sammy crawled next to Josh. This time someone saw him.

"A spider!" shrieked Shannon.

"I'm afraid of spiders," cried Gabby.

"Step on it!" yelled Jordan.

"Leave it alone," said Josh. "It can't hurt you. Don't you remember what Miss Sarah said? We have to be kind to animals."

"It's not an animal. It's a bug!" insisted Todd.

"We need to be kind to all creatures," said Miss Sarah.

Josh picked up Sammy. Seeing the little spider crawl across his hand made the other children less afraid.

"Can I hold him?" asked Jordan.

"Me, too?" Shannon asked cautiously.

"He tickles my hand," laughed Gabby, when it was her turn.

"It's time to let the spider go," said Miss Sarah.

Josh carefully carried Sammy outside and gently placed him on the ground. "Goodbye, little spider," he whispered. "Go home to your mother."

While the children washed their hands
for lunch, Sammy crawled back inside the
classroom and climbed into Josh's backpack.
"That was close," he thought. "I think I'd
better stay here until school is over."

On the ride home, Josh told his mother about the little spider.

"I'm proud of you, Josh," said Mrs. Shapiro. "You helped your friends understand what kindness to animals means."

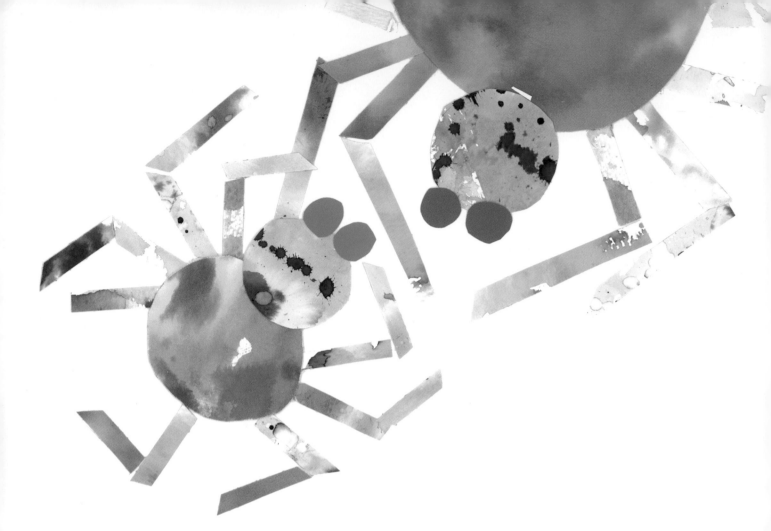

When Josh arrived home, he emptied his backpack. Sammy crawled out and hurried back to his web.

"How was your day at school?" asked Mrs. Spider.

"I made a lot of friends," announced Sammy. "They were very kind to me."

"Will you go back tomorrow?" inquired Mrs. Spider.

"Silly Mommy," he said. "Spiders don't go to school. Spiders spin webs."